Mama,
If You Had a Wish

Mama,
If You Had a Wish

By Jeanne Modesitt

Illustrated by Robin Spowart

ALADDIN PAPERBACKS

First Aladdin Paperbacks edition February 1999

Aladdin Paperbacks
An imprint of Simon & Schuster Children's Publishing Division
1230 Avenue of the Americas
New York, NY 10020

Printed and bound in the United States of America
10 9 8 7

The Library of Congress has cataloged the hardcover edition as follows:
Modesitt, Jeanne.
Mama, if you had a wish / by Jeanne Modesitt ; illustrated by Robin Spowart.
p.   cm.
Summary: If Little Bunny's mother could have one wish about her child,
it would be to keep Little Bunny unchanged and loved by her.
[1. Mother and child–Fiction.   2. Individuality–Fiction.
3. Rabbits–Fiction.   4. Wishes–Fiction.]
I. Spowart, Robin, ill. II. Title. PZ7.M715Mam 1993
[E]–dc20 91-31354 CIP ISBN 0-671-75437-8
ISBN 0-689-82412-2 (Aladdin pbk.)

To all of us.

"Mama," asked Little Bunny,
"if you had a wish,

would you wish I never cried?"

"No, Little Bunny," answered Mama,
"but it does make me sad
   to see you cry."

"Would you wish I was
    brave all the time, and never
got scared of anything?"

"No, Little Bunny," said Mama.
"We all get scared sometimes."

"What about when I get mad at you?"
asked Little Bunny.
"Would you wish I never did that?"

"No, Little Bunny," said Mama.
"I love you when you are mad at me,
and I love you when you are not."

"I bet I know what you would wish," said Little Bunny. "You would wish I never made any mistakes."

"No, Little Bunny," said Mama,
"I love you no matter how many
mistakes you make."

"Even big giant mistakes?"
"Even big giant mistakes."

"Well," said Little Bunny,
"you probably would wish I looked
different, wouldn't you?"

"No, Little Bunny," said Mama.
"I wouldn't wish you to look
any different than you do."

Little Bunny was quiet for a moment. "Mama, if you could make one wish about me, what would it be?"

"I would wish for you to be yourself," said Mama, "because I love you just the way you are."